D0995988

Turnaround

by

Alison Prince

MORAY COUNCIL LIBRARIES & INFO.SERVICES	
2O 2O 34 72	
Askews	
JCY	

First published in Great Britain by Barrington Stoke Ltd
10 Belford Terrace, Edinburgh EH4 3DQ
Copyright © 2002 Alison Prince

The moral right of the author has been asserted in
accordance with the Copyright, Designs and
Patents Act 1988
ISBN 1-84299-044-6
Printed by Polestar AUP Aberdeen Ltd

A Note from the Author

I live on a Scottish island, so it seems natural to set my stories in the same kind of place. Visitors are very much part of our lives in this small community, and they sometimes bring a touch of the unexpected with them.

The secret which lies at the heart of Kerry's family is a surprisingly common one. Drinking can be a pleasant, sociable thing, but it has a dark side. I've seen the effects of this in my own life, and know how children sometimes carry a burden of worry and fear. It's too embarrassing to talk about, and anyway, who would listen? Better to struggle on and pretend things are OK.

Unless something happens, as it does to Kerry, which changes the whole scene.

Contents

Chapter 1
Mum and Her Headaches

It's Saturday morning, half past nine.

I'm changing the sheets in the holiday cottage we let to visitors. It's a yucky job. I hate the scrunched up Kleenex under the pillows and those vile little bits of cotton wool covered with make-up in the bathroom.

Mum gives me a hand sometimes, but today she's got one of her headaches, so she's still in bed. I don't mind. I'm better on my own – Mum and I always seem to get in each other's way. Anyhow, in the school holidays, Dad pays me to do the turnaround, as we call it, which means cleaning the cottage and getting it ready for the next lot of people. It's my job, and I don't need any help.

I clean the kitchen sink and wipe the surfaces. The hob's the worst bit with all the burnt-on food.

Then I move into the bathroom. I clean the bath, basin and toilet, put fresh towels on the rails, empty the bin. Then vacuum everywhere, make sure the TV remote is on top of the set. It isn't. I hunt around for it, find it between the cushions on the sofa. Better than the half-eaten cheese sandwich I found last week – it's amazing what people will do.

Last of all, I go out and pick some sweet peas from the garden, and put them in a vase on the coffee table in the sitting room. I always do that, it's nice to make the place look welcoming. Then I pick up the pile of dirty sheets I've dumped by the door, and let myself out.

Our house is just down the path from the cottage, a big place built of red sandstone, looking out over the sea. That's one of the great things about living on an island, you get brilliant views everywhere.

Mum's come down. She's sitting at the kitchen table in her dressing gown, warming her hands round a mug of coffee.

"I'll come and help you in a minute," she says. "Soon as I'm dressed."

I tell her, "There's no need. It's all done."

She looks upset and says, "You could have waited."

"Sorry, Mum."

It's past twelve now, and the new people could be here at any minute if they've come over on the 10.20 a.m. boat. I had to get on with things. But I don't want to argue, it's never any good. I just say, "It doesn't matter, honest. I don't mind doing it alone."

Mum sighs. "You make me feel so useless," she says.

It's always like this. Nothing's ever right for Mum, and it's no good trying to cheer her up. If I tell her things are fine, she just gets angry and says I don't understand. And she's right, I don't.

Maybe it's her headaches. Sometimes I come home from school and find Mum lying on the sofa, feeling so ill that she hardly knows who I am.

She's usually better by the time Dad comes in, and she won't let me tell him she was flat out. She says he's got enough to worry about, running the business. He owns a building firm, and I must admit, he works incredibly hard.

I used to worry that Mum's headaches were a sign of something really bad, like a brain tumour, but she told me the doctor had done all the tests and couldn't find anything wrong. Just stress, she said.

I don't know why she's stressed. It's not as if she's got school exams to work for or a business to run. There's the shopping and cooking, but she's got her own car, and she mostly buys stuff that you just unwrap and microwave, so there's not that much work. I can't help wondering if there's something the doctor hasn't spotted – but I'd rather not think about it.

****

It's two o'clock and the next lot of visitors are here. Mum takes the key and goes up the path to the cottage with them, smiling and talking. She looks fine now. She's wearing jeans and a striped top and big, hooped earrings.

"I'm going to Gran's," I call after her, and she turns and waves.

"Right, sweetie, see you later!"

To look at her now, you'd never think she could be ill.

Chapter 2
The Shop

Ten to three now and I'm in Gran's shop. It's called *Second Time Round* because she sells secondhand stuff. It stands with its back to the sea, so it's always cool inside. Nice to come into when the sun is hot in the street.

The bell over the door tings when I go in. Gran is pulling stuff out of cardboard boxes by the counter, but she looks up and gives me her big smile.

"Hi, honey," she says. "You wouldn't believe the things people bring in. I mean, just look at this." She holds up a flat leather handbag that's so old, it's got green mould on it.

"I reckon they can't bear to throw it away because it was their old mum's or something," she adds. "So they bring it in here, and if I bin it, well, it's not *their* fault."

"You could be right," I say.

I love Gran's shop, because you never know what you'll find. There was a wicked dress last year, quite short, with a zigzag pattern in black and white. I wore it for my part in *The Boy Friend* when the school did it as their end-of-term show, and everyone said it looked dead cool.

There's something from the 1960s playing on the tape deck. Gran's got a CD player at home, but she has this old ghetto blaster in the shop. It's useful because people bring in secondhand tapes for sale, and she needs to know if they work. Sometimes they're all knotted up inside.

"What's this music?" I ask.

"The Beach Boys," Gran says. "I used to love their stuff." She waves her hands to and fro a couple of times as if she's dancing, then goes on fishing things out of the boxes.

"Chess set," she says, and hands me the wooden box. "Just check if all the pieces are there, Kerry. Now, what else is there? Plastic butter dish, toast rack."

She fits them in between the stuff that's already packed on the table, then gets out a Victorian cake stand.

"That'll sell," she says. "Now, what's this?" She opens a carrier bag and groans.

"Old socks. Does someone really think I can sell old socks?"

"You can sell anything," I say. I'm setting out the chess pieces on the counter beside the till because there's no board with them.

"*Almost* anything but not old socks," says Gran and she bungs the bag in the bin.

Dad's not keen on the shop. He can't see why his mother has to 'muck about with other people's rubbish', as he puts it. I think he feels a bit ashamed of her. His building firm is the biggest on the island, and he'd like Gran to ask him for anything she needs. She doesn't have to keep working, he says, not now. He'd be happy to buy things for her.

But I know she'd miss the shop and the people coming in. What would she do, sitting at home all day with no-one to talk to? There'd be no point in keeping her hair well cut and honey-blonde and wearing smart clothes. Even if most of them come from her shop, she always looks really good. She says if you're dealing with the public, it's important.

"How's your mum, Kerry?" asks Gran.

"OK."

Gran often asks, but I don't want to talk about it. What's the point?

"The chess men are all here," I tell her, and pack the pieces back in their box.

"Good," says Gran. "I'll get a fiver for those."

It seems a lot, when there's no board with them. But I expect she's right.

Chapter 3
An Awful Row

A week's gone by, and it's turnaround again. And I'm running late. It's not my fault – I got caught up in this awful row between Mum and Dad.

I hate rows. If I see there's going to be one, I get out of the way and leave them to it, but this morning it sort of crept up on me.

Dad was opening the post. He chucked most of it in the bin and kept one or two things, then he stopped over a letter and frowned. He pushed his chair back from the table and went into the hall, then shouted up the stairs, "Pat! Come down here, will you?"

There was no answer from Mum, of course. It was only half past nine, and she was still in bed. She hates mornings. She finds them hard to face, even if they don't start until midday.

I'd just made some toast, so I sat down and buttered it, never thinking for a minute that Mum would get up. But Dad went upstairs and did a lot more shouting about how he was sick of her lying in bed all morning, then came stumping down again.

He glanced at his watch then looked at me, and I thought it was a hint that I should be getting on with the turnaround.

"I'll go in a minute," I said, licking marmalade off my fingers.

Then Mum came down, knotting the tie of her dressing gown and looking puffy-eyed.

Dad pushed the letter at her and said, "What's all this?"

I saw then why he'd wanted me to leave. I picked up my toast and stood up, but Mum said, "Oh, Kerry, don't go. Please." She was hunched up like a sick bird.

I couldn't walk out after that, so I switched the kettle on, as if I'd just got up to make another cup of coffee.

Mum looked at the letter and said, "It's from Bidwell's."

That was the island's supermarket.

"It's a *bill* from Bidwell's," said Dad. "For £362. So what's been going on? Why have you been running up bills? You should pay them every time you go there."

Mum pushed her fingers through her hair and gave a sort of shrug. "Sometimes I didn't have my cheque book with me," she said.

Dad managed to keep his temper. "You don't use your cheque book for buying groceries. Why didn't you use our joint card?"

"I like to get a few little extras for myself," Mum said, looking sulky. "I don't know why they've bothered you with this silly bill. I told them I'd pay it."

"So what were these little extras?" Dad demanded. "I haven't noticed anything special. Seems to me you're still opening tins and shoving things in the microwave. Or are we talking about something else?"

Mum's eyes swam with tears. "You wouldn't notice whatever I did," she said. She can always talk and cry at the same time, I don't know how she does it.

Then she went ranting on and on. "I just don't matter, do I. You don't need me. I might as well be dead."

Dad looked at me and said firmly, "Kerry, you've got the turnaround to do, haven't you."

So here I am, sitting on the bed in the back room of the cottage, looking out at the hill. I ought to be getting on, but somehow I can't seem to move.

I wish my family could be just ordinary and cheerful, like my friend Jody's. They don't have money like we do, but they don't have rows, either, as far as I can see.

The top of the hill is hidden in cloud. There'll be no sun until it clears. I must stop sitting here, or the new people will be arriving before I've finished. *Get up*, I tell myself. *Get on*.

Chapter 4
Paul

Half an hour later and they're knocking at the door. Why haven't they gone to the house? Mum's supposed to give them the key and show them round. But I don't know what's happening in the house.

Switch off the vacuum cleaner, open the door. Why are they here so soon? A boy a bit older than me is standing on the path. He's 17 or 18, with fair hair. There's an older woman with him.

"Hi," he says. "Are we too early?" I gaze at him. Pale blue shirt with the sleeves rolled up, nice smile. And I'm in my oldest jeans and a shapeless T-shirt.

"No – it's all right," I say, but it isn't, of course. I'm only halfway through my cleaning.

The woman says, "We went to the house, but there seemed to be nobody in. We're the Carters, by the way. I'm Helen and this is my son, Paul. We're booked in here for a week."

"I'm Kerry. I'm so sorry, I can't think where everyone is."

We shake hands. I wish I wasn't looking such a mess.

"Could we leave our bags here for now?" Mrs Carter asks. "I know we're a bit early – we caught the seven o'clock boat this morning."

Talk about keen, I think. I smile at them and say that'll be fine, and they bring their stuff in from the car – a rucksack and a case, plus several plastic carriers from Bidwell's. They must have stopped to do some shopping when they got off the boat.

"Is it OK if we put the milk in the fridge?" Paul asks.

"Yes, sure." I take them into the kitchen – thank goodness I've cleaned in here.

"See you later," they say, and off they go. At least the sun's come out. With any luck, it'll be a fine day.

****

It's ten past one and the house is quiet. Dad's car isn't here. He'll have gone to the office, or else to the golf club. I put the sheets in the washing machine and turn it on, then go to look for Mum.

She's gone back to bed.

"Would you like a cup of coffee?" I ask. "Or some lunch? It's gone one."

She's lying on her side, staring at nothing. There's an empty glass beside her, a small, balloon-shaped one on a short stem. She'll have had a brandy – she says it calms her nerves. After a minute, she turns over and looks up at me. Her face is red and blotchy with crying.

"Am I such an awful person?" she asks.

"Of course you're not."

I sit down beside her and put my hand over hers, but I don't want to talk about this.

"Your dad thinks I am."

"No, he doesn't. He worries about you, that's all." I hate being pig in the middle. "Your headaches and everything. He just wants you to be well and happy."

Mum's eyes brim with tears again. "I wish I could be sure," she says.

I hand her a tissue, and she manages a watery smile. "Dear Kerry," she says. "What would I do without you? You're my only friend."

"I'll go and make some lunch," I say. "Just some salad and stuff. And you get up, OK?"

"All right." Her breath smells of the brandy she's drunk, but she seems a bit better.

****

Half past two now, and Mum says she's fine. In fact, she's turned a bit ratty, and tells me I don't need to hang round her all the time. It gets on her nerves.

Round six-ish, I phone my friend Jody, and we meet in the village and hang around, drinking Coke. Some more people from school come along, and we end up going back to Jody's house to watch a video, and Jody's mum cooks spaghetti for everyone. She grumbles a bit because there are so many of us, but she doesn't really mean it.

Chapter 5
Paul and Me

Sunday morning, five to ten and it's raining.

Dad's sitting at the kitchen table, reading the Sunday papers. Mum's up and dressed, standing by the toaster with her arms folded, waiting for it to pop up. She's not saying anything, and neither is Dad.

I grab some cereal, then break the silence to say I'm going to give Gran a hand in the shop. She opens on Sundays all through the summer, and it's always busy on wet days, because the tourists come in out of the rain.

"Have a nice time," Dad says without looking up from his paper. And Mum still doesn't say anything.

****

"Hi, honey," Gran says as usual. "Glad you've come."

Like I expected, the shop is crowded. I take over the till while Gran goes round chatting to people, though she's also watching that nobody nicks anything.

She was right about the chess set. A man pays a fiver for it quite happily, board or no board.

We're busy until lunchtime, and then the place empties a bit.

"Coffee break," says Gran.

She's just handed me a steaming mug when the door opens again and two more people come in. It's Paul and his mother. And I suddenly know I dreamed about Paul last night, standing on the path in his blue shirt, and my heart seems to miss a beat. I know I'm blushing.

"Hi," he says easily. "You seem to be everywhere."

I explain about this being Gran's shop, and ask if he'd like a coffee, but he shakes his head.

"No, thanks. We've just had one."

His mother spots the shelves of books and says, "Oh, great." She goes over to look at them, and I wonder what to say to Paul. He's probably dead bored.

"I'm sorry it's raining," I say, then wish I hadn't. What a stupid remark.

He smiles and says, "It's not your fault."

"I know." I can't seem to find any words. "I just meant, I hope it doesn't spoil your holiday."

"Oh, I don't think so," he says. "If you want sun *all* the time, you go to Spain or somewhere, don't you?"

"Suppose so. Is this the first time you've been here?" It's one of those landlady questions like Mum asks the visitors. Why can't I loosen up?

Paul says, "We came when I was a kid. Years ago. Mum's always wanted to come back. Happy memories and all that."

He's good at talking. I sip my coffee while he tells me he's just left school. He's going to university in the autumn, to study engineering.

He'll be in Glasgow, but he comes from Dundee.

"Engineering," I say. "It sounds kind of – heavy." I can't imagine him in overalls, doing greasy things with spanners.

Paul laughs and says I've got the wrong idea. "I'll be studying electronics and computing. What about you?" he adds.

"I've one more year to do at school. After that – I don't know really." There's the Mum problem. *You're my only friend*, she always says. I don't feel I can leave her. But I can't tell Paul that. "How did you decide on engineering?" I ask.

He shrugs. "Computers are the thing, aren't they. My dad was a bank manager but there's not many of them about now. Computers do it all. So I reckoned I'd better get to know about them."

"Makes sense." I wonder why his dad isn't with them on this holiday, but I don't ask. That's their affair. "We used to have a bank here," I tell him, "but they closed it three years ago. There's just the van now."

"Van?"

"Mobile bank van. Only it's not so good, because people have to stand outside and wait their turn. No fun when it's raining."

"What do you do for fun here, anyway?" he asks. "It must get pretty dead in the winter."

"Not really. We put on plays and concerts, and there's sporty things. Badminton – I like badminton. And dances."

Then he says, "I saw a poster for a dance in the Village Hall, Tuesday night. *A Family Dance*, it said. What's the family bit?"

"It just means it's for everyone," I explain. "Kids can come, too, even quite little ones. They all join in."

"Sounds a laugh. Do you fancy giving it a go?"

I try to sound casual. "If you like."

I hope I'm not still blushing. It's the first time a boy has asked me out. And Paul isn't a boy, not really, he's left school. He'll soon be a student.

"Great," he says. Then he goes over to join his mother at the bookshelves.

Chapter 6
The Dance

Monday night, about half past nine and I'm upstairs in my room.

I said I was going to have an early night, but that was just an excuse. I wanted to be on my own to think about today, and it's hopeless with the TV on and Mum and Dad sitting there. Specially when Mum tries to make bright remarks about the programmes and Dad doesn't answer.

Paul's mother went off with her rucksack and binoculars and camera this morning – I saw her walk past the house. She's into birdwatching. A few minutes later, Paul came to the back door and asked if I'd like to go for a walk.

Good thing Dad wasn't there – he'd have laughed at the idea of me walking. I never walk anywhere if I can help it, and he's promised I can have driving lessons the minute I'm 17. It's going to be my birthday present.

But anyway, Paul's not a walker, either – he just meant pottering down to the village.

We sat on the grass behind the paper shop, chucking stones in the sea and eating ice-cream cones as if we were little kids. He said he used to bite the end off, and his mum got cross because the stuff dripped down his shirt. I used to do that, too.

After a bit, we walked along the beach, and found a place where someone had made a dam across the stream that runs out from under the road.

It was half washed away, so we built it up again. By the time we'd finished, we'd made quite a deep pool. We had to leave it because the tide was coming in, but Paul said we'd improve it tomorrow.

Mum was out when we came back to the house. Her car wasn't there, so she'd probably gone shopping. I made some tuna sandwiches and we ate them on the lawn.

Paul's mother came in from her birdwatching thrilled to bits because she'd seen a golden eagle. She's really nice.

She works at a wildlife centre where kids go to learn about nature.

Tomorrow is the family dance. I can't wait.

****

It was just brilliant. Paul's a great dancer – my friends were dead jealous. When he went off to get drinks for everyone Jody said, "Aren't you the lucky one! He's just gorgeous."

There was disco dancing as well as Scottish stuff. The last dance was a smoochy one. Everyone was on the floor, and some of the dads had little kids half-asleep on their shoulders. The lights were low, and the mirror ball sent flickers over the wall and the ceiling. I'd been to family dances before, but this was different. Magic.

We walked home along the shore road, and Paul took my hand. The moon was making a bright path over the sea. We stopped, and he said, "It looks as if you could walk along it."

I said, "All the way to somewhere else."

He asked where I'd go if I could choose, but I didn't know. Better not to, or it would turn into somewhere real, and stop being a peaceful dream.

We walked on home, and the garden smelt of fresh grass because Dad had mowed the lawn. Light from the sitting room windows was shining across it. I knew Mum would be expecting me to go in, but I didn't tell Paul that.

We crossed the lawn, dodging the light, and went up to where the path leads up to the cottage behind the house. Then Paul said, "Thanks for a terrific evening." And he kissed me.

He makes me feel so safe. I wish he lived here, but he doesn't. He'll leave on Saturday to go back to Dundee, and I don't know what I'll do without him.

Chapter 7
Spoiling It

Why does Mum have to spoil everything? I suppose I ought to have gone in to say goodnight after the dance last night, but I was so happy, I was afraid she and Dad would notice and say something embarrassing.

Mum was in bed when Paul called for me this morning. That's pretty normal, so I didn't think about it. We went for a real walk, all the way up the glen to the waterfall, and I was amazed to find I enjoyed it. We came back down the forestry road, and we were really hungry by that time, so we had a toasted sandwich in the pier café.

We came back at about four. Mum must have been watching for me, because we'd only just turned in from the road when there she was, standing on the doorstep. "Kerry, I want a word with you!" she shouted.

Paul said, "See you later," and went on up to the cottage.

I followed Mum into the house. We'd only got as far as the hall when she turned to face me.

"What do you think you're up to?" She was fizzing with rage. "Showing off that you've managed to find yourself a boyfriend? Making sure everyone notices?"

"But I haven't ..."

"Don't you say a word!" she rushed on. "What about *me*? I had lunch ready for you, and I waited and waited. At three o'clock I cleared it all away." Her eyes were filling with tears. "You just don't care, do you. As long as *you're* having a good time."

When has she ever done lunch? Dad and I get ourselves a sandwich if we happen to be in, and Mum only eats when she feels like it, which isn't often. But she was crying good and proper now, so I didn't shout back, though it was hard not to.

I said I was sorry, but that didn't help, either. She sat down on the stairs with her head in one hand, groping for her hanky with the other.

I sat down beside her. I tried to put my arm round her, but she pushed me off. She got to her feet and stumbled up the stairs.

"I don't want your pity!" she shouted from the landing. "And don't stand there staring at me like some halfwit. Go and see your precious boyfriend – he'll be waiting." She went into her room and slammed the door.

I didn't go out, of course. She might have been watching through the window, and I couldn't risk that.

When Dad came in at six, he asked, "Where's your mother?"

I told him what had happened, and he sighed and said, "Why do you have to upset her?"

I said, "I didn't mean to."

Dad didn't answer. He was poking about in the fridge for something to eat. Then he gave up and said, "I'll get something while I'm out – I've got a golf club meeting. Will you be all right?"

"Yes," I said. "Fine."

I'm always fine. But this time I'm silently raging.

****

Thursday morning, about nine and Paul's at the back door.

"Hi," he says. He looks worried. "Your mum seemed a bit annoyed yesterday. Is it because of me? I mean, I wouldn't want ..."

"No, she gets like that." It's not the true answer, but Paul nods and doesn't ask any more. That's one of the things I love about him, he knows when to shut up.

We walk down the road and come to the boats for hire, pulled up on the beach by the village shop. He stops to look at them. Then he says, "Shall we give it a go? Could be fun."

I've never been out in one of the boats – we always think they're just for tourists. But why not?

"OK," I said.

And he's right, it is fun. He sits beside the little put-put motor and steers, and I trail a hand in the water. It's weird to look back across the widening gap of sea to the island. That's the place where I live, but I'm apart from it now. Our world is this little boat and the sea and the sky. *All the way to somewhere else.* This is what somewhere else should be like, full of nothing much, but shared with someone you trust.

Chapter 8
Disaster

We did mean to be back by lunchtime, we really did. But we were out in the boat for ages, and came back starving, so we went for steak pie and chips. Now we're walking back to the house, and I don't know what Mum's going to say.

At least she's not on the doorstep.

"See you at seven," Paul says, and goes off to the cottage.

I'm going to the play in the village hall with him and his mother – he said she suggested it this morning, before she went out.

I open the back door and go in. Mum's not in the kitchen. "Hi!" I call. "I'm back."

No answer.

I can hear the TV from the sitting room, so I go in.

She's lying on the floor, face down beside the sofa. I rush across. She's been sick, there's a pool of it soaking into the carpet. I try to lift her, but I can't – and maybe I shouldn't. I wish I knew more about First Aid.

I manage to roll her over, but her arm flops down heavily and I'm terrified she's dead. It's not new to find her flat out on the sofa, but I've always been able to wake her. This time I can't.

I'm out of the door, running up the path to the cottage. Paul's coming out of the door, he's seen me.

"It's Mum." I'm gasping for breath. "I don't know what's happened, she ..."

He's ahead of me, tearing back to the house.

Thank God, she's groaning a little, paddling around on the floor, trying to crawl. I grab tissues from a box and wipe her face.

Paul switches the TV off and says, "What's your doctor's number? I'll phone."

Mum manages to wave a hand. "No doctor," she mutters. "No."

We get her onto the sofa. She's shivering. Her eyes are shut, and she's hugging herself, head down on her knees.

"You need to be in bed," I say.

She doesn't answer.

Paul glances at me with his eyebrows up, and I nod.

"Come on," I say. "Up the stairs."

We help her to her feet and half carry her into the hall.

She sees the stairs and pushes us off. "I can manage," she says. But she can't, of course – she's all over the place. Somehow we get her up to the landing and into her room. She flops down on her bed. I take her shoes off and pull the duvet over her.

Paul's standing at the door. "Shall I make a cup of tea?" he asks.

"Coffee," Mum mutters.

We go down to the kitchen.

Waiting for the kettle to boil. Paul looks at me and asks, "What are you going to do?"

I shrug. "Take her some coffee. Then get the sitting room cleared up."

"Kerry," he says gently, "she's been drinking. There was an empty bottle on the table. And the smell ..."

I feel my face turn crimson. He shouldn't talk about things like that. Nobody should. We never do. And he's not right, anyway. "She has a brandy sometimes, it helps her relax." I'm angry with him. "She gets these headaches."

He goes on looking at me. His eyes are grey and very steady. "I think it's more than that."

I've turned my head away, I don't want to listen.

"I know it's not my business," he says. "If you want me to shut up and go away, I will. But, you see, it happened to my family as well."

"What did?" It sounds rude, but he goes on.

"I didn't tell you much about my dad. He lost his job, right enough, but it was because of the drinking. He was an alcoholic, you see. They could have found him another job when the branch closed, but they didn't. It's an illness, Kerry. And the longer you hide it, the worse it gets."

I'm staring at him in panic, as if something is slipping out of my hands and I can't stop it. An eggshell has smashed despite all my care. I can't breathe. The secret I've never put a name to is out. I won't be alone with it any more. I feel weak and shaky.

I give a very small nod. Then I'm crying and Paul's arms are round me.

"I know," he says. "It's tough. But it's not just you, or me and my mum. It happens to hundreds of people. Thousands."

I nod again. For some weird reason, I want to lie down somewhere quiet and go to sleep. But there are things to be done. I reach for a tissue and dry my eyes.

"Coffee," Paul says. He puts two heaped spoonfuls into a mug and pours the water on. "Black?"

"Yes. She never takes milk."

He puts the hot mug into my hand, and opens the door for me.

When I come back, I say, "She seems a bit better."

I'm not used to sharing the secret yet. I don't want to tell him how she clutched at me and went on about how I was her only friend and I mustn't say anything to Dad because he'll worry. All the same old stuff.

How can I tell Dad? He lives in a different world, dealing with work and money and machinery. If you ask me he thinks it's only weak people who have feelings. If they got their lives properly sorted out, they wouldn't need feelings. Weakness is something to be ashamed of. Something to hide.

Paul asks, "Does your dad know?" It's like he's guessed what I'm thinking.

I don't answer for a moment. Then I say, "He probably does."

The row over the Bidwell's bill must have been because she was buying booze. He always asks to see the till slips from the supermarket shopping.

Mum has always resented it. *Doesn't he trust me?* Well, no. He doesn't, and I can see why now.

Somebody walks past, outside the window. It's Paul's mother, with her rucksack and binoculars, on her way up to the cottage.

Paul sees her, too. "Oh, good," he says.

He sounds relieved. All this must have been quite heavy for him as well as me – I hadn't stopped to think about that.

He stands up from the table, then turns back. "Listen, Kerry, is it all right if I tell Mum what's happened? She'll understand. She's been through it herself."

I almost panic again. Once out, a secret runs so fast. But his mother will know about that. "Yes, you can tell her," I say. But there's one question I haven't asked. It's nagging me. "What happened to your dad? Is he – ?" But even as I ask, Paul's face tells me the answer, and my hands are over my mouth.

"My father died," he says. "Two years ago. His liver packed up."

"Oh, no. I'm so sorry, I shouldn't have said anything."

"Of course you should." He's frowning. "I ought to have told you in the first place. It's just – I don't talk about it much."

I nod. I can't imagine starting to talk about Mum. Paul's one thing, but the world is full of strangers.

"He wouldn't admit it," Paul says. "Always said there was nothing wrong, he was in control. But you mustn't worry, people do get over it. Lots of them." He glances out of the window, at the cottage.

I say, "I'll just go and check on Mum. See you later, OK?"

"OK," he says. I'll come back soon."

Then he opens the door and goes out.

Chapter 9
Afterwards

I'm lying in bed. It's late but I can't sleep for thinking about what happened today.

Mum had stopped shivering when I went to look at her. She was asleep, snoring a bit. I filled a glass of water and put it by her bed, then went down and cleared up the mess on the carpet.

I'd just finished when Paul came back. His mother was with him – she said to call her Helen. She was really nice.

She didn't say a lot, but she offered to stay in the kitchen if I wanted to go out and talk to my dad in his office. "If your mum calls out or needs anything, I'll hear her, and she knows who I am. So don't worry about leaving her."

It seemed a bit odd to go out when Mum was in bed. I never did, but this was a crisis. I didn't go and see Dad. He's never alone, there are always people in and out of the office, and I didn't know what I'd say to him, anyway. So I went to see Gran in the shop.

She took one look at me and asked, "What's happened?"

"It's Mum ..."

"Hang on," she said.

She went over to the last people in the shop, a couple who were dithering over a table lamp, and said, "I'm sorry, we're closing now." She gave them her big smile, and they went out like lambs.

Gran turned the notice in the door from 'Open' to 'Closed', then said, "Now, Kerry – tell me all about it."

So I did.

"Thank goodness for that," Gran said when I'd finished. "I've thought there was a problem for ages. I talked to your dad about it, but he said I was imagining things. He always hated being told anything he didn't want to know, even when he was a wee boy."

We talked for ages. Gran said she'd come round this evening.

"Might be best if you took yourself off to see a friend, love," she said. But I didn't have to organise anything, because I was going to see the play with Paul and his mum. Helen.

Even Paul calls her Helen when he speaks to her. I can't imagine calling my mum Pat.

As it turned out, Paul and I went on our own.

****

When I got back to the house after talking to Gran, Dad was there. He'd come home early and found Helen in the kitchen, and wasn't too pleased about it. But she told him what had happened, and she must have made him listen.

She'd gone back to the cottage by the time I came in, and Dad was standing by the sitting room window with his hands in his pockets, staring out at nothing much.

He turned to look at me and asked, "Where have you been?"

I said, "I went to see Gran."

"So you've told her – all about this?"

"Yes."

He wasn't happy about that, either.
"Why didn't you come to me? The office is no
further away than your gran's shop. How do
you think I feel, coming into my own house to
find a stranger in the kitchen who tells me
news like this?"

It's not news to you, I thought. But I didn't
say so, just shrugged and said, "I thought you
might be busy."

His shoulders seemed to sag and suddenly
I felt sorry for him. *How do you think I feel?*
he'd said. So he did have feelings, too.
He'd turned away to look out of the window
again. "What a mess," he said. "And now
you've told your gran, the whole world will
know."

I nearly said I was sorry, but I managed not to. We couldn't go back into secrets and pretending things were fine, not now.

"It's an illness," I said. "And Paul's father ..." I knew my voice was going to shake, and I couldn't go on.

"I know," said Dad. He's never been the hugging sort, but he put his hand on my arm. "Kerry – that's not going to happen to us."

I swallowed very hard. "It might," I said. They were only short words, but they sounded wobbly.

He did put his arms round me then, and held me close. "It won't," he promised. "We'll get lots of help. And we'll all have to think hard about how to put things right."

****

Mum came down a bit later, all bright and chatty, with freshly done make-up.

We had a silent meal of chicken curry from the microwave, then Paul came round and said Helen had decided not to go to the play, it would just be him and me.

When we came back, Mum and Dad and Helen were all in the sitting room, and so was Gran. We went and had a coffee in the cottage, and left them to it.

Chapter 10
Days that Lie Ahead

It's Friday morning, half past eight and Mum's up and dressed. Amazing. No make-up, though, so she looks very pale, and her eyes are puffy. She's made real coffee – she's pouring some for Dad, who's reading the paper. There are warm croissants, too, in the little bread basket. I hope she's dusted it, we haven't used it for ages.

Dad looks at the croissants and says, "What's this – instant France?"

"I just thought it would be nice," Mum says. "There were some in the freezer."

But Dad's run out of little jokes, so he just reaches for the butter.

****

Half an hour later, I'm stacking the breakfast things in the dishwasher. Dad's gone to work and Mum's wiping the table.

"So what are your plans for today?" She sounds bright and business-like, but it may not last.

"I don't know." Is she hoping I'll stay with her? Perhaps I ought to. But it's Paul's last day here – he goes home tomorrow.

The phone rings, and I pick it up.

"Hi, honey," says Gran. "Is your mum up yet?"

"Yes, she's right here, I'll pass you over."

Mum frowns as she listens, then says, "What, *today*?" She runs a hand through her hair. "Look, it's nice of you to bother, but honestly, I can deal with this on my own, I don't need …"

But Gran's talking again.

Mum sighs. "Oh, well, if you've fixed it. What time? Half past ten … I'll ask her." She looks at me. "Your Gran wants to know if you'll mind the shop for her this morning."

"Yes, of course." I don't know what Gran's up to, but I'll go along with it.

"She says she will," Mum reports. "See you later, then. All right. 'Bye."

She puts the phone down. "Your gran wants me to meet someone who runs a *group*. Honestly, I do wish people would mind their own business."

"But it *is* our business," I blurt out. I'm amazed to hear my own voice saying this. I've never argued with Mum, ever, just tried to keep her happy – but that's no good any more. "You're part of us, and we're part of you," I go on. "If you're not well, neither are we."

"Oh, Kerry, what a sweet thing to say." Her eyes swim with tears for a moment, but she wipes them away with her sleeve. Then she sighs. "But I'm so useless. Your dad's quite right, I'm a lousy housekeeper. And what else can I do? Nothing."

"But you can. You used to work before you were married, you told me. You were a chemist or something."

"I worked in a hospital. As a lab assistant."

"So there you are. You *could* get a job."

She shrugs, and I know she'll make excuses. She always does.

****

Mum went off with Gran to the group, not very happily, and Paul came with me to help mind the shop. He sold an amazing amount of stuff. He's not like Gran with the smile and the chat-up, just very polite and helpful, but it worked.

Gran didn't say much when she came back. When I caught her alone beside the kettle I asked, "How did it go?" and she just said, "Well, it's a start."

She insisted on giving us each a fiver for minding the shop. Paul didn't want to take it, but she said, "Don't be silly." And that was that.

We bought some picnic stuff, then walked up the path to the headland above the beach. It was great up there.

We sat on the rock and watched the seals swimming in the water. Sometimes they hauled themselves out and lay in the sun, enjoying it like we were. Lucky things. They'd never have to do anything else.

Paul wrote his address down for me. He said we'd keep in touch, and I just nodded. I was starting to run out of words again, like when we first met.

The thought of him going away was lying over me like a cold shadow, but I tried not to show it. Things had been heavy enough this week without me moping. And, as he said, he'll be in Glasgow when the university term starts. We can meet there sometimes, it's not as far away as Dundee.

We went to a jazz session later.
The players were all oldies except for Jamie
Burns who's in my form at school and plays
drums. It was a lot better than I'd expected.

Mum and Dad were both up when I got in,
watching TV. Mum made some tea and I told
them about the jazz, and we were all very
nice to each other. And careful.

****

Saturday morning and they've gone. At half
past seven this morning, I stood on the grass
by the cottage and waved goodbye as their
car went down the drive. I can still feel
Paul's light kiss and the grip of his hands,
giving me courage. "I'll see you soon," he said.
"Keep in touch."

So now it's another turnaround. Usually,
the departed visitors don't seem real to me,

but today, the cottage is still full of Paul and his mother. I've stripped the beds and I'm carrying the sheets downstairs.

Mum's coming through the door with a bucket. She's wearing an old shirt of Dad's, and her hair's tied back.

"I thought I'd do the windows," she says.

"Good idea."

We both go upstairs, Mum with the bucket and me with the vacuum cleaner. I plug it in and get going.

Mum looks pleased when she's done the first window. "That's better," she says. "Nice to have a clear view."

I switch the cleaner off. Outside, the cloud is lifting from the hill. It's going to be a sunny day. But I know the days that lie ahead won't all be sunny. We're going to have difficult times.

70

"There's a lot to do," I say.

Mum doesn't answer, just gives a little nod. Then she starts on the next window.

I empty the wastepaper basket.
There's nothing much in it, just a couple of used ferry tickets and a newspaper. Paul and his mother left things very tidy. But I dust the bedside table and clean the mirror, then move into the bathroom.

The turnaround always seems to take ages, but it's no good trying to rush it.

That's the way it is.

Barrington Stoke would like to thank all its readers for commenting on the manuscript before publication and in particular:

Kylie Barton
Anthea Beale
Elizabeth Benson
Alie Bishop
Ruth Black
Ann Carr
Christopher Clarke
Susan Cranfield
Mark Devereux
Kirsty Dewar
Vivian Faichney
Mike Falconer
Daniel Farmer
Kirsten Halter
Joseph Perry Hulme
Sue Hunt

Adil Islam
Christine Johnson
James Ketteringham
James Litster
William Milton
Carolyn Oakley
Liz Owens
Allan Page
Melanie Parker
Stephanie Pears
Paul Reilly
Wayne Taylor
Chris Walker
Liz Watson
Robert Young

Become a Consultant!

Would you like to give us feedback on our titles before they are published? Contact us at the e-mail address below – we'd love to hear from you!

E-mail: info@barringtonstoke.co.uk
Website: www.barringtonstoke.co.uk

More Teen Titles!

Joe's Story by Rachel Anderson 1-902260-70-8
Playing Against the Odds by Bernard Ashley 1-902260-69-4
Harpies by David Belbin 1-842990-31-4
TWOCKING by Eric Brown 1-842990-42-X
To Be A Millionaire by Yvonne Coppard 1-902260-58-9
All We Know of Heaven by Peter Crowther 1-842990-32-2
Ring of Truth by Alan Durant 1-842990-33-0
Falling Awake by Vivian French 1-902260-54-6
The Wedding Present by Adèle Geras 1-902260-77-5
Shadow on the Stairs by Ann Halam 1-902260-57-0
Alien Deeps by Douglas Hill 1-902260-55-4
Dade County's Big Summer by Lesley Howarth 1-842990-43-8
Runaway Teacher by Pete Johnson 1-902260-59-7
No Stone Unturned by Brian Keaney 1-842990-34-9
Wings by James Lovegrove 1-842990-11-X
A Kind of Magic by Catherine MacPhail 1-842990-10-1
Clone Zone by Jonathan Meres 1-842990-09-8
The Dogs by Mark Morris 1-902260-76-7
Dream On by Bali Rai 1-842990-45-4
All Change by Rosie Rushton 1-902260-75-9
The Blessed and The Damned by Sara Sheridan 1-842990-08-X

Barrington Stoke, 10 Belford Terrace, Edinburgh EH4 3DQ
Tel: 0131 315 4933 Fax: 0131 315 4934
E-mail: info@barringtonstoke.demon.co.uk
Website: www.barringtonstoke.co.uk